A Just Right Book

HOW MANY KISSES
Good Night

by Jean Monrad

illustrated by Eloise Wilkin

RANDOM HOUSE 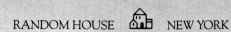 NEW YORK

Illustrations copyright © 1986 by Random House, Inc.
All rights reserved under International and Pan-American Copyright Conventions.
Published in the United States by Random House, Inc., New York, and simultaneously
in Canada by Random House of Canada Limited, Toronto.

Library of Congress Cataloging-in-Publication Data:
Monrad, Jean. How many kisses good night. (A Just right book)
SUMMARY: Questions in rhyme to ask a child at bedtime.
For example: "How many eyes? How many noses? How many fingers? How many toeses?"
[1. Bedtime—Fiction. 2. Stories in rhyme] I. Wilkin, Eloise Burns, ill.
II. Title. III. Series: Just right book (New York, N.Y.)
PZ8.3.M757Ho 1989 [E] 88-6453 ISBN: 0-394-88253-9

Manufactured in Singapore   6 7 8 9 0

JUST RIGHT BOOKS is a trademark of Random House, Inc.

How many eyes?

How many noses?

How many fingers?

How many toeses?

How many ears,

like roses curled?

And lips for the merriest
smile in the world?

How many tummies round?

How many teeth?

How many pink tongues

hiding underneath?

How many hairs
on your tip-top?

Is it millions?

Or hundreds,

or thousands,

or billions or trillions?

How many sheets
on your very own bed?

How many pillows
to comfort your head?

How many blankets
tucked round just right?
How many kisses to say...

Good Night